N/AP

D1268503

ST. LOUIS SCHOOL
FOND DU LAC, WIS

THE PIED PIPER OF HAMELIN

Retold by Catherine Storr
Illustrated by Anna Dzierżek

Raintree Childrens Books
Milwaukee • Toronto • Melbourne • London
Belitha Press Limited • London

Copyright © in this format Belitha Press Ltd, 1984
Text copyright © Catherine Storr 1984
Illustrations copyright © Anna Dzierżek 1984
Art Director: Treld Bicknell

First published in the United States of America 1984
by Raintree Publishers Inc.
205 West Highland Avenue, Milwaukee, Wisconsin 53203
in association with Belita Press Ltd, London.

Conceived, designed and produced by Belitha Press, Ltd
40 Belitha Villas, London N1 1PD

ISBN 0-8172-2107-7 (U.S.A.)

Library of Congress Cataloging in Publication Data

Storr, Catherine.
  The Pied Piper.
  Summary: The Pied Piper pipes the village free of rats and when the villagers refuse to pay him for the service, he pipes away their children, too.
  1. Pied Piper of Hamelin—Legends.   2. Legends—Germany (West)—Hameln.   3. Hameln (Germany)—History—Juvenile fiction.   [1. Pied Piper of Hamelin.   2. Folklore—Germany.   3. Hameln (Germany)—History—Fiction]
I. Dzierżek, Anna, ill.   II. Title.
PZ8.1.S882Pi   1984   398.2'1'0943   83-26971
ISBN 0-8172-2107-7

All rights reserved. No part of this book may be reproduced or utilized in any form or by any means, electronic or mechanical, including photocopying, recording, or any information storage and retrieval system, without permission in writing from the Publisher.

Cover printed in the United States; body printed in Great Britain.
Bound in the United States of America.

There is a little town in Germany called Hamelin. The River Weser runs by its south wall. Several hundred years ago the people living there were having a terrible time. . . .

The trouble was . . . RATS! There were hundreds and thousands, tens of thousands of them. They were bold rats, hungry rats, thieving rats. They fought dogs, they killed cats. And they ate everything. They made nests in all sorts of unlikely places. And as the townspeople sat at meetings, or talked with their neighbors and played with their children, they could hear the rats squeaking and gibbering and fighting under the floorboards and behind the walls.

5

At last it became more than they could bear. The townspeople marched off together to find the Mayor of Hamelin and his Council. They stormed into the Town Hall and began to speak their minds. "What use are you," they cried, "if you can't get rid of these rats for us? Why should we pay for you to have these grand clothes and that great gold chain? All you do is sit here talking and eating grand dinners at our expense. You don't do anything to help us."

The Mayor and his Council were
shocked. They sat for a long time,
discussing what they could do. But no
one had any useful suggestions, and they
felt gloomier and gloomier. "It's a desperate
situation," the Mayor said at last. "I'd sell
my gold chain and my grand robes if
anyone could find a way of getting rid of
this plague of rats. But I don't believe there
is anyone who could do that."

He had hardly finished speaking when there was a knock on the door of the Council Chamber. A voice asked, "May I come in?"

C ome in," the Mayor said. The person who opened the door and stood in front of the Mayor and his Council was very strange to look at. He was tall and thin, with a shock of light hair and bright, twinkling blue eyes. He wore a long coat, half red and half yellow, and around his neck was a red and yellow scarf. The Mayor and his Council stared, and the stranger's eyes twinkled more than ever as he saw their astonishment.

He walked right up to the Council table. "Please, your Honor," he said, "listen to me. I have a secret charm by which I can make any living creature follow me, wherever I go. I often use this magic to rid the people who hire me of harmful creatures, like snakes and mice and cockroaches. Everyone knows me as the Pied Piper." As he said this, he pulled out the end of his scarf, and the Mayor saw that it was tied to a little wooden pipe.

"You see this pipe?" the strange man said. "This holds my secret magic. I have been all over the world with this, helping people to get free of creatures that plague them. I was in Tartary not long ago, freeing the Great Cham of a swarm of gnats. Then I went to India to get rid of a brood of vampire bats that was annoying the Nizam. I cleared a plague of locusts from one of the African countries. It would be easy for me to get rid of your rats for you, but . . . you will have to pay me a thousand guilders."

"Only a thousand? We'll give you fifty thousand if you can really do that!" exclaimed the Mayor with joy.

13

The Pied Piper smiled. Then he stepped out into the street and put the pipe to his lips. Before he had played more than a few notes, there was another sound in the street—a very different sound. It was not music; it was the sound of excited squeaks and mutterings. It was the sound of the patter of a million tiny clawed feet. The rats were leaving the houses and the cellars and the barns and the sheds, and they were running to follow the music of the pipe.

Whole families, whole clans, an army of rats were enchanted by the music, and they danced after the Piper down the street that led to the river Weser. As he reached the river's edge, the Piper suddenly stood still. But he continued to play on his pipe, and the rats rushed past him, leaped over him, tumbled over themselves, and fell into the deep water. And they were drowned, dead.

15

All but one. One rat swam across the river and reached the other side. Much, much later, he told the story to his great grandchildren. "When I heard the music of the pipe," he said, "I heard other sounds, far more exciting. I heard apples being put into the press to make cider. I heard cupboard doors creak open and stay open for me to get at the food inside. I heard corks being drawn out of oil jars, and the scraping of the covers off huge, ripe cheeses. I heard a voice calling, sweeter than any music. 'Rats, rejoice!' it said. 'Come and eat as much as you can hold; the feast is spread.' So I ran with the others, and then, suddenly, I found myself in the river, with water nearly over my head."

You should have heard the rejoicing of the people of Hamelin when they discovered that the rats had really gone! They rang the church bells till the steeple rocked. They poked out the rats' nests. They cleaned out all the messes, and as they worked they sang and cheered.

But, suddenly, the Pied Piper appeared in the marketplace and said, "Now, please pay me my thousand guilders!"

A thousand guilders!" said the Mayor, as if he were surprised. He thought about all the good dinners he could buy with the money. He thought about the bottles of rare wines he had in his cellar and about the money he would need to buy more. "This strange fellow can't bring the rats back again. They're all safely drowned in the river," the Mayor said to his Council.

To the Piper he said, "A thousand guilders! You must be joking. I don't mind giving you something so that you can buy yourself a drink, but we've lost so much because of the rats that I couldn't possibly give you a thousand guilders. Take fifty!"

The Piper's expression changed. "Don't try to joke with me," he said. "Keep to the bargain, and be quick about it. By dinner time I've got to get back to Baghdad, where the Sultan's cook is making a feast for me. I routed out a nest of scorpions in his kitchen and he paid me well. I'm not going to haggle with you, you shifty little man. Give me my thousand guilders, or I'll play my pipe in a way you won't like at all."

The Mayor grew angry. "Do you think I'm going to be treated worse than a cook? I won't be insulted by a ridiculously-dressed strolling player! You won't get a penny from me. Go on! Blow your silly pipe till you burst!"

The Piper did not answer. He raised his pipe to his lips again, and this time the music that he played was the sweetest anyone had ever heard. And at once there came the sound of small feet running, of wooden clogs clattering along the street.

There came, too, the sound of little voices whispering and calling to each other. Then the horrified Mayor and his Council saw the children. All the children of Hamelin were hurrying out of the houses to join the Piper. And as he strode down the street, the children ran after him, never turning to look back.

The Mayor and his Council stood speechless, as if they had been turned to stone. They saw the Piper go toward the river and wondered if he was leading the children to drown like the rats. But the Piper walked on, beside the river, toward a great mountain that stood outside the town, and the frantic mothers and fathers, who were stumbling after their children, breathed more easily again. "He'll have to stop when he reaches the mountain. Then the children will come back to us," they said.

But when the Piper reached the mountain, a door opened in the hillside, and the Piper went in, still piping. The children followed, and the door shut behind them.

Only one child was left behind. He was lame and had not been able to keep up with the others. When he was brought back to the town, he told what the Piper's music had said to him. "The pipe said that the Piper was leading us to a magical land where there were springs of fresh water and trees filled with fruit.

"It said that the flowers there were even better than here. The birds are more brightly colored, the honeybees never sting, and there are winged horses for us to ride. Now all the other children are in that wonderful place, but I'm left here alone, with no one to play with."

The Mayor sent messengers out—east, west, north, and south—to try to find the lost children. He offered great rewards of gold and silver. But no one had seen anything of the Pied Piper, nor of the children who had followed him.

Every year since then, the day in July when the children disappeared has been a day of mourning. The street leading to the mountain was called the Pied Piper's street. A great stone column was built near the hillside where once the door had opened into the mountain. And on the column was written the whole story—so that no one would forget the Pied Piper and the stolen children.

31

It has been said that in the mysterious country of Transylvania there are families of people who look quite different from their neighbors. The story is told that hundreds of years ago the ancestors of these families escaped from an underground prison where they had been trapped. When they were asked where they had come from, they said they thought they had once lived in a town called Hamelin. But how they had got from Hamelin to the prison, or from the prison to Transylvania, they could not remember or ever explain.